Anne
of
Green Gables

Don't miss L. M. Montgomery's *Emily of New Moon,*
adapted by Priscilla Galloway.

And for the complete story of Anne, look for these
books in your bookstore or library:

Anne of Green Gables

Anne of Avonlea

Anne of the Island

Anne of Windy Poplars

Anne's House of Dreams

Anne of Ingleside

Rainbow Valley

Rilla of Ingleside

Anne of Green Gables

by
L. M. Montgomery

Adapted by Shelley Tanaka

SEAL BOOKS

"Anne of Green Gables" and other images of "Anne" are trademarks and
Canadian official marks of the Anne of Green Gables Licensing Authority Inc.
which is owned by the heirs of L.M. Montgomery and the Province of Prince
Edward Island and located in Charlottetown, Prince Edward Island.

"L.M. Montgomery" is a trademark of the Heirs of L.M. Montgomery Inc.
used under license by Seal Books.

Seal Books and colophon are trademarks
of Random House of Canada Limited.

This edition contains the complete text of the original hardcover edition.
NOT ONE WORD HAS BEEN OMITTED

ANNE OF GREEN GABLES
Seal Books / Published by arrangement with Delacorte Press

Delacorte Press hardcover edition published March 1988 /
Seal Books edition published simultaneously

Book design by Patrice Sheridan

ISBN: 0-7704-2744-8

Seal Books are published by Doubleday Canada, a division of
Random House of Canada Limited. "Seal Books" and the portrayal of a seal,
are the property of Random House of Canada Limited.

Visit Random House of Canada Limited's website: www.randomhouse.ca

PRINTED AND BOUND IN THE USA

BVG   10 9 8 7 6 5 4 3

With special thanks to
Carl Bernard, Jeff Karkheck, Eric Moniz, Danielle Pixley,
and Kayla Roblin
at the Prince Charles School in Napanee, Ontario

Contents

Chapter 1

𝒯𝒯atthew Cuthbert Is Surprised

Mr. Matthew Cuthbert was late. Anne had been waiting for him for more than half an hour outside the train station at Bright River. He was coming to take her to Green Gables, her new home.

"If he doesn't come for me," Anne said to herself, "I'll climb that big cherry tree. It would be lovely to sleep among its white blossoms under the moonshine."

Just then a gray-haired man shuffled down the platform toward her. He seemed almost surprised to see her.

Anne stood up quickly and held out her hand.

"Are you Mr. Matthew Cuthbert of Green Gables?" she said in a clear, sweet voice. "I was worried that you weren't coming for me."

"I'm sorry I'm late," the man said shyly.

"Come along. The horse and buggy are in front of the station."

"I'm so glad I'm going to live with you," Anne said as they drove out of the village. "My parents died when I was a baby, and since then I've never belonged to anybody. Oh, look at the trees all in bloom! This island is the bloomiest place. I just love it already. Mrs. Spencer is the lady who brought me here from the orphanage. She said Prince Edward Island is the prettiest place in the world, but I never dreamed I would ever live here."

Matthew said nothing. He looked down at Anne's eager face. She was smiling up at him. She was a thin, gray-eyed girl of eleven. She wore a very tight, ugly dress. Two thick red braids hung down her back. Her face was small and pale, with many freckles.

"Right now I feel almost perfectly happy," she said. "Of course, I can't really feel perfectly happy because, well . . ." Anne twitched one of her long braids over her thin shoulder. She held it in front of Matthew's eyes and asked, "What color would you call this?"

"It's red, isn't it?"

Anne uttered a sigh that seemed to come right from her toes.

"Yes," she said. "It's red. That is why I can never be perfectly happy. I don't mind being freckled and skinny so much. I can imagine that I have beautiful skin and blue eyes. But I can't imagine away my red hair, and it breaks my heart. It means I will never be beautiful. Which would you rather be if you had the choice? Divinely beautiful or dazzlingly clever or angelically good?"

"Well, now, I . . . I don't know."

"Neither do I. I can never decide. It doesn't really matter, because I'll probably never be any of them. But am I talking too much? People are always saying I do. Would you rather I didn't talk? I *can* stop when I make up my mind."

"You can talk as much as you like," Matthew said.

"Oh, I'm so glad. It's such a relief not to be told that children should be seen and not heard. I've had that said to me a million times. And people laugh at me because I use big words. But if you have big ideas, you have to use big words to express them, don't you?"

"Well, now, that seems reasonable."

"Mrs. Spencer said your place is named Green Gables. She said there are trees all around it. I just love trees. There were only a few teeny-weeny ones around the orphanage. They looked just like poor orphans themselves. I felt like crying whenever I looked at them.''

At that moment the buggy rounded a curve. Two rows of blossoming apple trees made an arch over the road ahead. At the far end the sunset shone like a huge pink window at the end of a cathedral aisle.

Anne hardly breathed as the buggy passed through the lovely tunnel of blossoms. Then she whispered, ''What was that white place?''

''People call it the Avenue,'' said Matthew. ''I guess it is kind of pretty.''

''They shouldn't call that wonderful place the Avenue. When I don't like the name of a place or a person, I always imagine a new one. From now on I will call it the White Way of Delight.''

The buggy drove over the top of a hill. Below them lay the village of Avonlea.

Anne looked carefully over the little valley dotted with tidy farmhouses. Finally she pointed to a white house that stood far back from the road.

''That's Green Gables, isn't it?'' she said.

''How did you guess?'' Matthew asked. ''Did Mrs. Spencer describe it?''

''No, but as soon as I saw it, I felt it was home.''

Matthew didn't say a word. He just turned the buggy into the long lane of Green Gables and drove up into the yard.

Anne was very quiet as she clutched her bag and followed him into the house.

Chapter 2

$\mathscr{M}$arilla Cuthbert Is Surprised

Matthew's sister, Marilla, was waiting for them. She was a thin, elderly woman who wore her hair pulled tightly away from her face in a bun.

"Matthew Cuthbert, who is this?" she exclaimed. "Where is the boy?"

"There wasn't any boy," Matthew said unhappily. "There was only *her*."

"But we told the orphanage we wanted to adopt a *boy*."

Anne looked up at the two grown-ups. Suddenly she understood what they were saying.

"You don't want me!" she cried. "You don't want me because I'm not a boy! I should have known it was too beautiful to last. Nobody ever did want me!" And she burst into tears.

Matthew and Marilla looked at each other. Neither of them knew what to say.

"Well, now, there's no need to cry about it," Marilla said finally.

"Yes, there *is*!" Anne raised her tear-stained face. "What if you were an orphan? What if you had come to a place you thought was going to be home and found that they didn't want you because you weren't a boy? Wouldn't you cry, too? Oh, this is the most *tragical* thing that has ever happened to me!"

"Well, don't cry anymore," Marilla said. She seemed to be trying not to smile. "Tell me your name."

"Will you please call me Cordelia?"

"Is that your name?"

"No, not exactly. But I would love to be called Cordelia. It's such an elegant name."

"I don't know what on earth you mean. If Cordelia isn't your name, what is?"

"Anne Shirley. But please call me Cordelia instead. Anne is such an unromantic name."

"Fiddlesticks!" said Marilla. "Anne is a good, plain, sensible name. You shouldn't be ashamed of it."

"I'm not. I just like Cordelia better. But if you must call me Anne, will you please call me Anne spelled with an *e*?"

"What difference does it make how it's spelled?" asked Marilla.

"Oh, it makes such a difference. *A-n-n* looks dreadful. *A-n-n-e* looks so much nicer."

"Very well, Anne spelled with an *e*. Can you tell us how this mistake happened? Were there no boys at the orphanage?"

"Yes, but they said you wanted a girl. If I was very beautiful and had brown hair would you keep me?"

"No. We have no use for a girl. Matthew is getting older and he has trouble with his heart. We need a boy to help him on the farm. Now let's sit down to supper. We're not going to turn you out-of-doors tonight."

But Anne could not eat. She nibbled at her bread and butter. She pecked at the crab apple preserves.

"You're not eating anything," Marilla said sharply.

Anne sighed.

"I can't. I'm too sad. In fact, I'm in the depths of despair. Can you eat when you're in the depths of despair?"

"I've never been in the depths of despair, so I can't say," replied Marilla.

"Well, did you ever try to *imagine* you were in the depths of despair?"

"No, I did not."

"Well, it's a very uncomfortable feeling. When you try to eat, a lump comes right up into your throat. You can't swallow anything, not even a chocolate caramel. I had a chocolate caramel once, two years ago. It was simply delicious. I don't want to be rude. Everything is very nice, but I still can't eat."

"I guess she's tired," said Matthew. "You should put her to bed, Marilla."

Marilla lit a candle and Anne followed her upstairs. She looked around at the room where she was to sleep. In one corner was a high, old-fashioned bed. In the other corner was a small table. Above it hung a little mirror. Between the table and bed was the window, and opposite it was a washstand.

The whole room was very clean and bare. Anne shivered. She put on her thin nightgown and sprang into bed. Then she buried her face in the pillow.

Marilla picked up the candle and went over to the bed.

"Well. Good night, then," she said, not unkindly.

Anne's white face and big eyes suddenly appeared over the blankets.

"How can you call it a good night?" she said. "This is the very worst night I've ever had." Then she slid down under the covers and cried herself to sleep.

Chapter 3

Marilla Makes Up Her Mind

Anne opened her eyes and sat up in bed. For a moment she did not know where she was. Then she remembered. This was Green Gables, and they didn't want her because she wasn't a boy!

But she couldn't stay sad for long. It was morning, and a flood of cheery sunshine was pouring through the window.

Anne jumped out of bed and looked out. A huge cherry tree, white like a snow queen, stood outside the window. On both sides of the house was a big orchard, its trees covered with flowers. The grass beneath them was sprinkled with dandelions. The sweet smell of lilacs drifted up to the window on the morning breeze.

"It's time you were dressed," said Marilla as she walked into the room.

"Don't you just love the world on a morning

like this?'' Anne said. ''I can even hear a brook out there. Have you ever noticed how cheerful brooks are? They're always laughing. I'm not in the depths of despair this morning. I've been imagining that you really wanted to keep me after all, and that I'm going to stay here forever. But the worst thing about imagining is that in the end you have to stop. Then it hurts.''

''Never mind your imaginings,'' said Marilla. ''Get dressed and come downstairs for breakfast. Then we will drive over to White Sands and see Mrs. Spencer. We have to decide what to do about this mix-up.''

Later that morning Marilla and Anne drove off in the buggy. Matthew leaned on the gate and watched them go. He looked very sad.

The road to White Sands followed the shore. On one side stood a thick forest of fir trees. On the other were steep red cliffs that tumbled down to the sea. Seagulls soared overhead. Their wings looked like silver in the sunlight.

Anne sighed. ''You know,'' she said, ''I've decided to enjoy this drive. I can almost always enjoy things if I firmly make up my mind to. I am not going to think about going back to the orphanage. I am just going to think about the drive.''

''As long as you're going to talk, you might as well tell me about yourself,'' Marilla said.

''Oh, my life isn't really worth telling about,'' said Anne. ''Let me tell you what I *imagine* about myself. It's so much more interesting.''

''Just stick to the facts. How old are you?''

''I was eleven last March,'' said Anne with a little sigh. ''My mother and father died when I was a baby, and I had no other relatives. Nobody wanted me, but finally Mr. and Mrs. Thomas took me in. I helped look after the four Thomas children who were younger than me. Then Mr. Thomas was killed when he fell under a train. His mother offered to take Mrs. Thomas and the children, but she didn't want me. So Mrs. Hammond took me, because I was handy with children. She had twins three times. I used to get so tired carrying them around. Then Mr. Hammond died and I had to go into the orphanage. I was there for four months until Mrs. Spencer came.''

No wonder the child was so happy at the thought of a real home, Marilla thought. But she said nothing.

⁓

Mrs. Spencer was surprised to see Marilla and Anne standing at her door.

"There's been a mistake," Marilla said. "Matthew and I wanted you to bring us a boy."

"But I thought you wanted a girl!"

"Well, we didn't. Can we send the child back?"

"I suppose so," said Mrs. Spencer thoughtfully. "But I don't think that will be necessary. Mrs. Blewett was here yesterday. She's looking for a child to help her. She has a large family, you know. Anne will be the very girl for her. And here comes Mrs. Blewett now!" she exclaimed. "We can settle the matter right away."

Anne stared at the sharp-faced, thin woman who was marching up the lane. A lump came into her throat.

"There's been a mistake about this little girl, Mrs. Blewett," said Mrs. Spencer. "I thought the Cuthberts wanted to adopt a girl, but it seems they wanted a boy. So this child may be just the thing for you."

Mrs. Blewett darted her eyes over Anne from head to foot.

"Humph! There's not much to you. But you're wiry, and the wiry ones can work the hardest. You'll have to be good and smart and respectful. I'll expect you to earn your keep. All right, I can take her home right now, Miss Cuthbert.''

Marilla looked down at Anne's pale, miserable face.

''Well, I don't know,'' she said slowly. ''I didn't say that we were absolutely not going to keep her. I just wanted to find out how the mistake happened. I think I'll take her home again and talk it over with Matthew. If we decide not to keep her, we'll bring her back tomorrow.''

Anne did not speak until she and Marilla were in the buggy, driving back to Green Gables.

''Oh, Miss Cuthbert,'' Anne whispered. ''Did you mean it? You might let me stay with you?''

''I haven't decided yet,'' Marilla said crossly. ''Mrs. Blewett certainly needs you more than I do.''

''I'd rather go back to the orphanage than live with that woman,'' Anne said firmly. ''I'll do anything you want, if only you'll keep me.''

⸺

The next day, when Anne had finished washing the breakfast dishes, she approached Marilla. Anne was trembling from head to foot.

''Please, Miss Cuthbert. Won't you tell me

whether you are going to send me away? I've tried to be patient, but I cannot bear it any longer.''

''Well, I suppose I might as well tell you. Matthew and I have decided to keep you. But you must be good and . . . why are you crying?''

''I don't know,'' Anne said. ''I'm so happy. Oh, I'll try so hard to be good. It will be uphill work, I expect, but I'll do my very best.''

''Well, sit down and try to calm yourself. I'm afraid you both cry and laugh far too easily.''

''Can I call you Aunt Marilla?'' asked Anne. ''That would make me feel as if I really belonged to you.''

''You'll call me just plain Marilla. I'm not your aunt and I don't believe in calling people names that don't belong to them.''

''But you could imagine you were my aunt.''

''No, I could not,'' Marilla said grimly.

''Don't you ever imagine things different from what they really are?'' Anne asked, her eyes wide.

''No.''

''Oh, Marilla,'' Anne said, ''how much you miss!''

That evening Anne went up to her room and sat by the window. She looked around at the plain walls and began to imagine things into the room. In her mind, the floor was covered with a white velvet carpet with pink roses all over it. Pink silk curtains hung at the window. She imagined that her small looking glass was a huge mirror, and that she herself was Lady Cordelia Fitzgerald, with beautiful midnight-black hair.

Anne went up to the little looking glass. She peered into it. A pointed, freckled face peered back at her.

"I'm not Lady Cordelia," she said to her reflection. "I'm just Anne of Green Gables. But I don't mind one bit. It's a million times nicer being Anne of Green Gables than Anne of nowhere in particular."

Chapter 4

Mrs. Rachel Lynde Is Horrified

Soon after Anne arrived at Green Gables, Rachel Lynde came to visit. She was a plump, outspoken woman who liked to keep a close eye on everybody in the village. She had heard that the Cuthberts had adopted a girl, and she was very curious to meet Anne.

Mrs. Lynde settled herself in the kitchen and shook her head with disapproval.

"You don't know a single thing about this strange child," she told Marilla. "Why, just last week I read about a man and his wife who adopted a boy. He set fire to the house and nearly burned them to a crisp in their beds."

Just then Anne came running in. She had been playing in the orchard, and her hair was ruffled and windblown. It had never looked redder.

She stopped shyly when she saw that Marilla had a visitor.

"Well, they didn't pick you for your looks, that's for sure," said Mrs. Lynde. "You're terribly skinny. Goodness, did you ever see such freckles? And hair as red as carrots!"

Anne bounded across the kitchen floor and stood in front of Mrs. Lynde. Her whole body trembled.

"I hate you!" she cried in a choked voice. "How dare you call me skinny and ugly? You are a rude, unfeeling woman!"

"Anne!" exclaimed Marilla.

But Anne wasn't finished.

"How would you like to be told that you are fat and probably haven't a spark of imagination in you? I don't care if I do hurt your feelings by saying so. You have hurt mine worse than they have ever been hurt before. And I'll never forgive you for it!"

"Anne, go to your room and stay there until I come up," Marilla ordered.

Anne burst into tears and rushed out of the room. She slammed the door so hard that the tins on the shelf rattled.

"You shouldn't have said those things about her looks, Rachel," Marilla said.

"Marilla Cuthbert, are you defending such a terrible display of temper?" Mrs. Lynde demanded.

"No," said Marilla. "She's been very rude and I'll have to speak to her about it. But she's never been taught what is right. And you *were* too hard on her."

Mrs. Lynde stood up stiffly. "Well, I see that I'll have to be very careful what I say after this. I had no idea that the feelings of orphans, brought from goodness knows where, have to be considered before anything else. Goodbye, Marilla. I hope you'll come down to see me as usual. But don't expect me to visit here again."

And with that, Mrs. Lynde waddled out the door.

Marilla went upstairs. Anne lay facedown on her bed. She was crying bitterly.

"Anne," Marilla said. "Get off that bed this minute."

Anne squirmed off the bed and sat on the chair. Her face was swollen and tear-stained.

"She had no right to call me ugly and redheaded," she told Marilla.

"You had no right to talk to her the way you did. I

was ashamed of you. Besides, you often say yourself that you are red-haired and ugly.''

''But there's such a difference between saying it yourself and hearing other people say it,'' cried Anne. ''You may know a thing is true. But you can't help hoping other people don't think it is. When she said those things, something just rose up in me and choked me. I couldn't help it.''

''Well, Mrs. Lynde will have a nice story to tell about you now. It was very rude to lose your temper like that.''

''Just imagine how you would feel if somebody told you that you were skinny and ugly,'' Anne said tearfully.

Marilla was silent for a moment. Then she said gently, ''I'm not saying Mrs. Lynde was right. But she was a stranger and an older person and my visitor. Those were three very good reasons why you should have been respectful to her. Now you must go and tell her you are very sorry. You must ask her to forgive you.''

''I can never do that,'' Anne said. ''You can shut me up in a dark, damp dungeon full of snakes and toads. I won't complain. But I cannot ask Mrs. Lynde to forgive me.''

"Dungeons are rather scarce in Avonlea," Marilla said. "But you'll stay here in your room until you're ready to apologize."

"Then I will have to stay here forever," Anne said. "How can I tell Mrs. Lynde I'm sorry when I'm not? I can't even *imagine* I'm sorry."

"Well, perhaps your imagination will be working better in the morning," said Marilla. "You said you would try to be good if we kept you at Green Gables. Well, you haven't been a very good girl today. You'll have the night to think it over."

All the next day Anne stayed in her room. Marilla brought her meals on a tray, but Anne ate very little.

That evening when Marilla went out to bring in the cows, Matthew tiptoed upstairs. He tapped on the door to Anne's room and peeped in.

Anne was sitting by the window. She looked very small and unhappy.

"Anne," Matthew whispered. "How are you?"

Anne smiled bravely.

"Pretty well. I imagine a good deal, and that helps

to pass the time. Of course, it's a little lonely, but I might as well get used to it.''

''Well, now, Anne. Marilla's very determined. Don't you think you'd better get it over with?''

''You mean apologize to Mrs. Lynde?''

''Yes. Just smooth it over, so to speak.''

''I suppose I could do it for you,'' Anne said thoughtfully. ''It would be true enough to say I'm sorry, because I *am* sorry now. I wasn't a bit sorry last night. I was mad clear through, and I stayed mad all night. I know I did because I woke up three times, and I was just furious every time. But this morning it was all over. I felt so ashamed of myself. But I just couldn't think of going and telling Mrs. Lynde. Still, I'd do anything for you—if you really want me to . . .''

''Of course I do. It's terribly lonely downstairs without you.''

''Very well,'' said Anne. ''I'll apologize.''

''That's a good girl. But don't tell Marilla I said anything. She might think I was interfering, and I promised not to do that.''

''Wild horses won't drag the secret from me,'' Anne promised.

⌒

That evening, as the sun was setting, Anne and Marilla walked down the lane to Mrs. Lynde's house. Rachel Lynde was sitting by her kitchen window.

Anne went down on her knees in front of Mrs. Lynde and held out her hands.

"Oh, Mrs. Lynde, I am so sorry," she said. Her voice quivered a little. "I could never say how sorry I am, not if I used up a whole dictionary. I behaved terribly to you, and I've disgraced Matthew and Marilla, who have let me stay at Green Gables even though I'm not a boy. Every word you said was true. My hair *is* red, and I'm freckled and skinny and ugly. What I said to you was true, too, but I shouldn't have said it. Oh, Mrs. Lynde, won't you please, please forgive me?"

Anne clasped her hands together and bowed her head.

Mrs. Lynde looked a little startled. "Well, of course I forgive you, child," she said. "I guess I was too hard on you. You mustn't mind me. I once knew a girl whose hair was every bit as red as yours. Then when she grew up, it darkened to a handsome reddish brown. I wouldn't be surprised if yours did, too.''

''Oh, Mrs. Lynde!'' Anne drew a long breath as she rose to her feet. ''You have given me hope. Now may I go out and sit on that bench under the apple trees while you and Marilla are talking? There is so much more room for imagination out there.''

''Yes, run along. And you may pick a bouquet of white June lilies if you like.''

As the door closed behind Anne, Mrs. Lynde got up to light a lamp.

''She's an odd child, and her temper's pretty quick. But a child with a quick temper just blazes up and then cools down. She isn't likely to be sneaky or dishonest. On the whole, Marilla, I kind of like her. She may turn out all right.''

When Marilla was ready to go home, Anne came out of the orchard with a bouquet of white flowers in her hands.

''I apologized pretty well, didn't I?'' she said proudly as they walked down the lane. ''I thought since I had to do it, I might as well do a thorough job.''

''You were thorough, all right,'' Marilla replied.

"But I hope you won't need to make many more such apologies. Please try to control your temper now, Anne."

"That wouldn't be so hard if people didn't tease me about my hair," said Anne with a sigh. "It just makes me boil right over. Do you suppose my hair *will* get darker when I grow up?"

"You shouldn't think so much about your looks. I'm afraid you are a very vain little girl."

"How can I be vain when I know I'm not pretty?" protested Anne. "When I look in the mirror I feel so sad—just the way I feel when I look at any ugly thing. I feel sorry for it because it isn't beautiful." Anne smelled her flowers. "Wasn't it nice of Mrs. Lynde to give these to me? I have no hard feelings against her now. It gives you a lovely, comfortable feeling to apologize and be forgiven, doesn't it?"

Far up in the shadows, a cheerful light gleamed through the trees. It was coming from the kitchen at Green Gables. Anne suddenly slipped her thin little hand into Marilla's.

"It's lovely to be going home and know it's home," she said. "I love Green Gables already, and I've never loved any place before."

Chapter 5

⁓

*A*nne Meets Diana

"Well, how do you like them?" asked Marilla, as she spread three new dresses out on Anne's bed. "I made them myself."

Anne held up one of the dresses. It was very stiff, with black and white checks.

"I guess I can imagine that I like them," she said slowly.

"But what is the matter with them? Aren't they clean and new?"

"Yes."

"Then why don't you like them?"

"They're not pretty."

"Pretty!" Marilla sniffed. "I didn't worry about making them pretty. These are good sensible dresses, and they're all you'll get this summer. I'll expect you to keep them neat and clean. You should be grateful to get them."

"Oh, I am," said Anne. "But I'd be so much gratefuller if you'd made just one of them with puffed sleeves. Puffed sleeves are so fashionable now. It would give me such a thrill to wear a dress with puffed sleeves."

"Well, you'll have to do without your thrill. I don't believe in wasting material on puffed sleeves. They look ridiculous. I prefer the plain, sensible ones."

"I'd rather look ridiculous when everybody else does than plain and sensible all by myself," Anne said.

"Trust you to feel that way," said Marilla crossly. She started to go downstairs and then paused. "By the way, I'm going over to borrow a skirt pattern from Mrs. Barry. The Barrys live nearby on Orchard Slope. If you like, you can come with me and meet their daughter Diana. She's about your age."

Anne rose to her feet. The dress she had been holding slipped to the floor.

"Oh, Marilla, what if she doesn't like me? It would be the most tragical disappointment of my life."

"I wish you wouldn't use such long words. It sounds so funny in a little girl. I'm sure Diana will like you well enough. It's her mother you've got to worry about. She is very strict with her children. If she doesn't like you, it won't matter how much Diana does. I hope Mrs. Barry hasn't heard about your outburst to Mrs. Lynde and how you went to church last Sunday with roses and buttercups stuck all over your hat. I should have known better than to send you by yourself, even if I did have a terrible headache. What a ridiculous sight you must have been!''

"Lots of girls had flowers pinned on their dresses," said Anne. "Why is it any more ridiculous to wear them on your hat?''

"Don't answer me back like that, Anne. It was a very silly thing to do. Now, you must be polite and well behaved when we visit the Barrys. And for goodness' sake, stop trembling.''

Anne's face was pale and tense.

"You'd be nervous, too, if you were going to meet the girl you hoped would be your best friend and whose mother might not like you. When I lived with Mrs. Thomas, she had a bookcase with glass doors. I used to pretend that my reflection was another little girl who lived inside. I called her Katie. I used to tell her everything. But I've never had a real live friend.''

Marilla and Anne took the shortcut across the brook to Orchard Slope. Mrs. Barry came to the door to meet them. Diana was sitting on the sofa, reading a book. She was very pretty. She had black hair, rosy cheeks, and a merry smile.

Mrs. Barry introduced the girls to each other. Then she said, "Diana, why don't you show Anne your flowers? It will be better for you than straining your eyes over that book. You read too much. Perhaps having someone to play with will get you outdoors more."

Out in the garden, Anne and Diana gazed shyly at one another.

"Oh, Diana," said Anne at last. "Do you think you will like me enough to be my best friend?"

Diana laughed.

"I guess so," she said. "It will be so much fun to have somebody to play with. No one else lives near enough, and my sister is too small."

"Will you swear to be my friend forever and ever?"

Diana looked shocked.

"But it's very bad to swear," she said.

"Not this kind of swearing. There are two kinds, you know."

"I've only heard of one kind," said Diana.

"The kind I mean just means promising solemnly."

"Well, I don't mind doing that," agreed Diana. "How do you do it?"

"We take each other's hands," Anne said. "It should be over running water, but we'll just imagine this path is running water. I'll say the promise first. I swear to be faithful to my best friend, Diana Barry, as long as the sun and moon shall endure. Now you say it and put my name in."

Diana did as she was told. Then she laughed.

"I heard that you were a strange girl, Anne, but I think we're going to get along really well."

When Marilla and Anne went home, Diana walked with them as far as the log bridge. The two girls promised to spend the next afternoon together.

"Oh, Marilla," Anne sighed. "I'm the happiest person on Prince Edward Island. Diana's birthday is in February and mine is in March. Don't you think that's an amazing coincidence? Diana's going to lend me a book to read. She's going to show me a place in the woods where wild lilies grow. Then we're going to the beach to gather shells and—"

"Well, I hope you won't talk Diana to death," said

Marilla. "And remember you're not just going to play. You'll have your chores to do first."

Anne didn't think she could be any happier—until Matthew got home from the store.

"I heard you say you liked chocolate sweeties, so I got you some," he said, handing a small package to Anne.

"Humph," sniffed Marilla. "It will ruin your teeth. Don't make yourself sick eating them all at once."

"Oh, I won't," Anne said. "I'll just eat one tonight. And I'll give half of them to Diana. The other half will taste twice as sweet to me if I give some to her."

Chapter 6

⁓

The Missing Brooch

That summer Anne and Diana played together every day. They made a wonderful playhouse in the woods. They used big stones for seats. For shelves, they propped boards between trees. On the shelves were bits of broken dishes that they had rescued from the woodshed.

One afternoon Anne came flying into the kitchen. Her eyes were shining with excitement.

"There's going to be a Sunday school picnic next week," she told Marilla. "In the field beside the Lake of Shining Waters. That's our new name for Mr. Barry's pond. Mrs. Lynde is going to make *ice cream*! I've never tasted ice cream. Diana tried to explain what it's like, but I guess ice cream is one of those things that are beyond imagination. Oh, Marilla, can I go?"

"What time did I tell you to come in, Anne?"

"Two o'clock. But can I go to the picnic? I've never—"

"Look at the clock. It's quarter to three. When I tell you to come in at a certain time I mean that time and not three-quarters of an hour later. As for the picnic, I wouldn't refuse to let you go when all the other little girls are going."

"But Diana says everybody must take a basket of things to eat. I don't mind going to a picnic without puffed sleeves so much, but I'd feel terrible if I had to go without a basket, and—"

"Don't worry. I'll fill a basket for you."

"Oh, Marilla, you are so good to me. Thank you." Anne threw herself into Marilla's arms and kissed her thin cheek. "I never believed I would ever go to a picnic."

"Now, never mind your kissing nonsense," Marilla said briskly. "You set your heart too much on things, Anne. I'm afraid there will be a great many disappointments in store for you."

"But looking forward to things is half the fun!" Anne exclaimed. "You may not get the things themselves, but nothing can stop you from looking forward to them."

Two days before the picnic Marilla came down-stairs. Her face was troubled. Anne was shelling peas in the kitchen.

"Anne," Marilla said, "have you seen my amethyst brooch? I put it on my bureau when I came home from church yesterday. Now I can't find it."

"I . . . I saw it this afternoon when you were out," said Anne a little slowly. "I was passing your door and I saw it on the bureau. I went in to look at it."

"Did you touch it?" asked Marilla sternly.

"Y-e-e-s," admitted Anne. "I pinned it on just to see how it would look."

"You had no business doing that. You shouldn't have gone into my room in the first place, and you shouldn't have touched a brooch that didn't belong to you. My mother gave me that brooch. Where did you put it?"

"I put it back on the bureau. I only had it on for a minute, but I see now I shouldn't have done that. I'll never do it again. That's one good thing about me. I never do the same bad thing twice."

"The brooch isn't anywhere on the bureau."

"But I put it back," Anne said quickly.

"Well, I'll go and have another look," said Marilla. "If you did put it back, it will be there."

Marilla went to her room and made a very thorough search. Then she returned to the kitchen.

"Anne, the brooch is gone. Now, tell me the truth. What have you done with it?"

"I never took the brooch out of your room and that is the truth. So there," Anne said.

"I don't believe you, Anne," Marilla said sharply. "No one else has been in that room. Don't say another word unless you're prepared to tell me the whole truth. Now go to your room."

All through the evening and the next day, Marilla searched for the brooch. She moved the bureau, took out all the drawers, and looked in every crook and cranny. But she didn't find it.

That night Marilla went to Anne's room again.

"You'll stay in this room until you confess, Anne," she said firmly.

"But the picnic is tomorrow," Anne cried. "You won't keep me from going to that, will you? Just let me out for the afternoon. Then I'll stay here as long as you like. But I *must* go to the picnic."

"You're not going anywhere until you've confessed, Anne," Marilla said. Then she walked out of the room and shut the door.

———

The day of the picnic was perfect, sunny and bright.

Marilla took Anne's breakfast to her. She found Anne sitting on the bed, her lips shut tight.

"Marilla, I'm ready to confess."

Marilla put down the tray. "Then let me hear what you have to say."

Anne cleared her throat and began to speak.

"I took the brooch," she said. "I pinned it on. Then I went down the road to the Lake of Shining Waters. On the bridge I took off the brooch to look at it gleaming in the sunshine. When I was leaning over the bridge, it slipped through my fingers and sank forevermore beneath the water. And that's the best I can do at confessing, Marilla."

"Anne, this is terrible," Marilla said. She was trying not to show how angry she was.

"Yes, I know," Anne agreed. "And I know I'll have to be punished. So will you please get it over with because I'd like to go to the picnic with nothing on my mind.''

"You're not going to any picnic today, Anne Shirley," Marilla said loudly. "That will be your punishment. And it isn't nearly severe enough for what you've done!"

Anne sprang to her feet. "Not go to the picnic!" she cried. "But you promised I could. That's why I confessed. Punish me any other way but please, please let me go to the picnic. Think of the ice cream. I may never have a chance to taste ice cream again."

"It's no use begging, Anne. You are not going and that's final."

When Anne realized Marilla wasn't going to change her mind, she gave a piercing shriek. Then she flung herself onto the bed, sobbing with disappointment.

～

Anne stayed in her room all morning. She cried and cried until she was all cried out. Then she sat by her window and gazed out sadly.

Shortly after noon the door to her room burst open. Marilla stood there. In her hands was her best lace shawl—and the brooch.

"Anne Shirley," Marilla said solemnly. "I've just found my brooch hanging on this shawl. Now I want to know why you told me that nonsense this morning."

Anne sighed loudly. "You said you'd keep me here until I confessed," she said. "So I did. I tried to make up the best story I could. But you wouldn't let me go to the picnic after all, so all my trouble was wasted."

Marilla couldn't help laughing.

"Oh, Anne, you do beat all. But I was wrong. I shouldn't have doubted your word. It was wrong to confess to a thing you hadn't done, but I drove you to it. So if you'll forgive me, I'll forgive you. Now get yourself ready for the picnic."

Anne flew up like a rocket.

"Isn't it too late?"

"It's only just started. Wash your face and comb your hair. I'll fill a basket for you."

Several hours later a perfectly happy, completely tired-out Anne returned to Green Gables.

"I've had an absolutely scrumptious time," she told Marilla. "First we had a splendid picnic lunch. Then six of us went rowing on the Lake of Shining

Waters. Jane Andrews leaned out to pick water lilies, and she nearly fell overboard. If her father hadn't caught her by her sash, she'd have fallen in. Wouldn't it be romantic to be nearly drowned? It would be such a thrilling tale to tell.''

Chapter 7

A Tempest in the School Teapot

"Isn't it good just to be alive on a day like this?" Anne said one splendid September morning. She and Diana were walking to school together. They took a pretty shortcut through the orchard, down the hill, and along the brook.

Anne breathed in the spicy scent of spruce trees. "I feel sorry for the people who aren't born yet. They may have good days, of course, but they'll never have this one."

Diana was busy examining her lunch. She had three juicy raspberry tarts in her basket today. She sighed when she realized that she would only get one or two bites. The girls in school always shared their lunches. Three tarts did not go far when they were divided among ten girls.

At noon all the girls ate and played together in the woods behind the school. They put their bottles of milk in the brook to keep cool. They made bead rings, played ball, and read stories to each other under the fir trees.

The Avonlea school was a cozy one-room building with a big blackboard on the front wall and a round black heating stove at the back. Anne and Diana shared an old-fashioned wooden desk. Each student had a little slate blackboard and chalk to practice his or her handwriting and arithmetic problems.

Anne had not gone to school regularly before she came to Green Gables, and she loved going. The schoolmaster, Mr. Phillips, was not a very good teacher, but Anne was smart. It didn't take her long to catch up on all the work she had missed.

"Gilbert Blythe will be in class today," said Diana. "He's been away visiting his cousins in New Brunswick. You'll have some competition now, Anne. Gilbert's used to being at the head of the class."

As it turned out, Gilbert sat across the aisle from Anne. He was tall, with curly brown hair and a teasing smile.

Anne watched as Gilbert carefully took Ruby Gillis's braid and pinned it to the back of her seat. When Ruby tried to stand up to answer a question, she fell back into her seat with a shriek. Mr. Phillips glared. But by that time Gilbert had removed the pin and was innocently studying his history book.

When the excitement had died down, Gilbert looked over at Anne and winked.

Anne turned away quickly and looked out the window. Gilbert frowned. He was not used to being ignored.

He reached across the aisle and grabbed the end of Anne's long red braid. Then he said in a piercing whisper, "Carrots! Carrots!"

Anne sprang to her feet and glared at Gilbert with angry eyes.

"How dare you!" she exclaimed. Then she brought her slate down on Gilbert's head with a giant *thwack* and broke the slate in two.

Everyone gasped.

Mr. Phillips came down the aisle. He put his hand heavily on Anne's shoulder.

"Anne, you will stand at the front of the class for the rest of the day."

"It was my fault, Mr. Phillips. I teased her," Gilbert said, but Mr. Phillips ignored him.

With a white, determined face Anne went to the

front of the room. Then Mr. Phillips wrote on the blackboard above her head: *Ann Shirley has a very bad temper. Ann Shirley must learn to control her temper.*

Anne stood and faced the class all afternoon. Her cheeks were red with shame and anger, but she did not cry.

When school was finally dismissed she marched out with her head held high. Gilbert was waiting for her outside the door.

"I'm sorry I made fun of your hair, Anne," he said. "Please don't be mad." But Anne swept by as if she hadn't even heard him.

"Gilbert makes fun of all the girls," Diana said, hurrying after her. "He calls me a crow all the time because my hair is so black. He's never said he was sorry for it once, either."

"Being called a crow is quite different from being called Carrots," Anne said. "Gilbert Blythe has hurt my feelings *excruciatingly,* and I will *never* forgive him."

Chapter 8

—

Diana Is Invited to Tea

October was a beautiful month at Green Gables. The birch trees in the hollow turned as golden as sunshine. The wild cherry trees along the lane were beautiful shades of dark red and orange.

Anne loved the world of color around her.

"I'm so glad I live in a world where there are Octobers," she said to Marilla one Saturday morning. "It would be terrible if we just skipped from September to November. Look at these bright red maple branches. I'm going to decorate my room with them."

"You clutter up your room too much with outdoors stuff, Anne. Bedrooms were made to sleep in."

"But they're made for dreaming in, too. And you can dream so much better in a room where there are pretty things. I'm going to put these in the old blue jug and set them on my table.''

"Well, don't drop leaves all over the stairs. I'm going to a church meeting this afternoon. I won't be home before dark. If you like, you can ask Diana to come over for tea.''

"What a wonderful idea!'' Anne said. "It will be so nice and grown-uppish. Can I use the good rosebud tea set?''

"No. You'll use the regular brown dishes. But you can serve the cherry preserves with fruitcake and cookies. And there's a bottle of raspberry cordial on the second shelf of the sitting room cupboard. You and Diana can drink some of that if you like.''

That afternoon Diana came over. She was wearing her second-best dress. Instead of running into the kitchen as usual, she knocked primly at the front door. After Anne opened it the two girls shook hands politely.

"How is your mother?'' Anne asked, even though she had spoken to Mrs. Barry that very morning.

"She is very well, thank you. Have you picked many of your apples yet?''

"Oh, ever so many.'' Anne suddenly forgot to be dignified as she grabbed Diana's arm. "But Marilla says we can have whatever is left. Let's go out and pick some before tea.''

The girls spent most of the afternoon in the orchard. They ate apples and talked as much as they could. Then they went into the house, and Anne looked for the raspberry cordial.

There was no bottle on the second shelf of the cupboard. Eventually she found it way back on the top shelf. She poured Diana a large glassful.

''I love bright red drinks, don't you?'' she asked. ''They taste twice as good as any other color.''

Diana sipped her drink daintily.

''This is awfully nice,'' she said. ''I didn't know raspberry cordial tasted so good.''

''Take as much as you want. I'm going to run out to the kitchen and put on the tea. There are so many things to do when one is keeping house.''

When Anne came back from the kitchen, Diana was drinking her third large glassful.

''This is so much nicer than Mrs. Lynde's, and she brags about hers so much.''

''Well, Marilla *is* a famous cook. She is trying to teach me to cook, too, but it isn't easy. There's so little room for the imagination when you're cooking. You just have to go by the rules. The last time I made a cake I forgot to put the flour in, and flour is quite important in cakes, you know. Why, Diana, what's the matter?''

Diana stood up unsteadily. Then she sat down again and put her hands to her head.

"I'm . . . sick," she said slowly. "I have to go home right now."

"But you can't go home before we have tea!"

"I have to go home," Diana repeated, and that was all she would say.

"Oh, Diana," Anne said, "do you suppose you're coming down with a horrible disease? If you are, I'll nurse you back to life, even if I get sick myself and die. Where do you feel bad?"

"I'm awfully dizzy."

Anne was overcome with disappointment. But she had no choice except to walk Diana back to her house.

—

The next day Marilla sent Anne down to Mrs. Lynde's on an errand. In a very short time Anne came flying back up the lane. Tears were rolling down her cheeks.

"What has gone wrong now, Anne?" asked Marilla. "I hope you haven't been rude to Mrs. Lynde again."

"Mrs. Lynde saw Mrs. Barry today," Anne wailed. "Mrs. Barry says I made Diana *drunk* yesterday. She says she's never going to let Diana play with me again."

Marilla stared in amazement.

"Made Diana drunk? What on earth did you give her?"

"Just your raspberry cordial," sobbed Anne. "But I never thought raspberry cordial would make someone drunk, not even three big glassfuls!"

Marilla marched to the sitting room cupboard and picked up the bottle on the shelf.

"Anne, you certainly have a genius for getting into trouble," she laughed. "You gave Diana currant wine. Don't you know the difference?"

"I never tasted it," said Anne. "Diana got awfully sick, and when her mother asked her what was wrong, she just laughed. Mrs. Barry smelled her breath and knew she was drunk. She thinks I did it on purpose."

"She should punish Diana for being greedy enough

to drink three large glassfuls of anything. Don't cry, Anne. Mrs. Barry will change her mind. Just go over later and tell her what really happened.''

—

That evening Anne stepped out into the cool autumn air. She walked through the clover field and up the hill to Orchard Slope.

Mrs. Barry opened the door.

''What do you want?'' she said.

''Oh, Mrs. Barry, please forgive me,'' Anne said. ''I did not mean to make Diana drunk. How could I? She's my best friend in the whole world. I thought I was serving her raspberry cordial. Please don't say you won't let Diana play with me anymore.''

''I don't think I want Diana to be friends with someone like you,'' Mrs. Barry said coldly. ''You'd better go home.'' And she went in and shut the door.

—

Mrs. Barry was true to her word. She allowed the girls ten minutes to say goodbye. Then she ordered Diana not to talk to Anne ever again, even in school.

The two friends exchanged locks of hair and promised to be friends forever.

"Please see that Diana's hair is buried with me," Anne told Marilla, "for I don't believe I'll live very long. Maybe when Mrs. Barry sees me lying cold and dead, she will feel sorry for what she has done. Perhaps she will let Diana come to my funeral."

School was the only thing left in Anne's life, so she threw her heart and soul into her studies. All fall she and Gilbert Blythe competed to be first in the class. One month Gilbert was three marks ahead. The next month Anne beat him by five.

She was determined not to be outdone by Gilbert Blythe. In fact, she had decided to hate him to the end of her life.

Chapter 9

$\mathcal{A}$nne to the Rescue

In January the prime minister of Canada came to Prince Edward Island. Many people in Avonlea went to the capital city of Charlottetown to hear him speak. Marilla, Mrs. Lynde, and Mr. and Mrs. Barry all made the overnight trip.

At Green Gables Anne and Matthew settled in for a cozy evening. A bright fire glowed in the kitchen stove. Frost crystals shone on the windowpanes. Matthew dozed and read, and Anne studied at the kitchen table. She tried not to think of the new book Jane Andrews had lent her. She couldn't wait to read it, but Gilbert would get ahead for sure if she didn't concentrate on her schoolwork.

Suddenly they heard footsteps on the porch. The kitchen door flew open, and in rushed Diana Barry.

"Come quick," Diana begged. Her face was white with fear. "My little sister is sick with the croup. My parents are away and there's nobody to go for the doctor. Oh, Anne, I'm so scared!"

Without a word Matthew reached for his hat and coat and headed out to the barn.

"He's gone to harness the horse to go for the doctor," Anne said, grabbing her jacket.

"But Dr. Blair and Dr. Spencer both went to town to hear the prime minister. What are we going to do?"

"Don't cry," Anne said calmly. "I know exactly what to do for croup. Mrs. Hammond had twins three times, and they all had croup regularly."

Anne grabbed a bottle of medicine, and the two girls hurried out into the frosty night.

Three-year-old Minnie May was very sick. She had a high fever, and her hoarse breathing could be heard all over the house.

Anne went right to work. She gave Minnie May medicine and bathed her hot body. All night long the child tossed and coughed, until Anne thought she might choke to death. But finally the medicine worked, and Minnie May began to breathe more easily. By the time Matthew arrived with the doctor, she was sleeping quietly.

It was morning when Anne and Matthew finally went home. Anne could hardly keep her eyes open. She fell into bed at once and didn't wake up until that afternoon.

Marilla was in the kitchen when Anne came down.

"Mrs. Barry was here earlier, Anne," she said. "She wanted to see you, but I wouldn't wake you up. Dr. Spencer told her that you saved Minnie May's life. Mrs. Barry says she knows now that you didn't mean to make Diana drunk. She hopes you'll forgive her and be good friends with Diana again. You're invited over now, if—"

But Anne didn't hear another word. She was already racing over to Orchard Slope, her red hair streaming behind her.

Chapter 10

A Concert and a Catastrophe

"Marilla, can I go over to see Diana just for a minute?" Anne asked one February evening.

"Why do you need to see her now? You and Diana walked home from school together. Then you stood in the snow for more than half an hour, your tongues going clickety-clack the whole time."

"But Diana has something important to tell me," pleaded Anne.

"How do you know?"

"Because we send messages to each other from our windows. We put a candle on the windowsill. Then we signal each other by passing a piece of cardboard in front of it. It was my idea."

"I'm sure it was. You'll soon set fire to the curtains with this nonsense."

"Oh, we're very careful. And it's so interesting. Diana has just signaled five flashes. That means I must go over to her house as soon as possible because she has something very important to tell me."

"Well, you can go, but be back here in ten minutes."

Anne came back bursting with news. The next day was Diana's birthday. Her cousins were coming to Avonlea to go to an evening concert at the town hall. They had invited Diana and Anne to go with them. Afterward Anne would spend the night at Diana's.

"Oh, I'm so excited," Anne said.

"Well, you can calm down then, because you're not going. You'll sleep at home in your own bed. You're not staying out at all hours of the night. I'm surprised that Mrs. Barry is letting Diana go."

"But it's such a special occasion," said Anne. She was on the verge of tears. "Diana only has one birthday a year. Mrs. Barry even said we could sleep in the guest room bed. Just think what an honor that would be for your little Anne."

"Well, it's an honor you'll have to do without. Now, take off your boots and go to bed. It's past eight."

The next morning Anne was washing the breakfast dishes in the pantry. She could hear Matthew and Marilla talking in the kitchen.

"I think you ought to let Anne go, Marilla," Matthew said.

"We agreed that I would bring her up, Matthew. You promised not to interfere."

"It isn't interfering to have an opinion."

Anne held her breath. For a long time there was no sound from the kitchen.

Finally she heard Marilla say, "Very well, she can go."

Anne flew out of the pantry. Greasy water dripped from her dishcloth onto the floor, but she didn't notice.

"Do you mean it, Marilla?" she asked.

"This is Matthew's doing. I wash my hands of it. If you catch cold coming out of that hot hall in the middle of the night, don't blame me!"

That afternoon Anne went home with Diana after school. The girls had a perfectly elegant tea. Then they got dressed for the concert. They experimented with different hairstyles and rearranged their bows at least a dozen times.

The cousins arrived in a big sleigh, and Anne and Diana crowded in. They drove to the Avonlea Hall, gliding over the satin-smooth snow. The sounds of sleigh bells and distant laughter grew louder as they drew near the hall.

The whole evening was like a beautiful dream. The choir sang, and speakers recited wonderful poems. Only one number on the program failed to interest Anne. She read a book during Gilbert Blythe's performance. Then she sat stiffly while the rest of the audience applauded loudly.

It was eleven o'clock when the girls were dropped off. The Barry house was dark and silent. Everybody seemed to be asleep.

Anne and Diana tiptoed into the parlor next to the guest room. They quickly put on their nightgowns.

"Are you ready?" Anne whispered. "I'll race you to the bed."

The two white-clad figures flew across the floor and through the guest room door. They bounded onto the bed.

Then something moved beneath them.

"Merciful goodness!" it cried.

In a frantic rush Anne and Diana jumped off the bed and ran out of the room.

"Who *was* that?" whispered Anne as they tiptoed upstairs.

"It was Aunt Josephine," said Diana, gasping with laughter. "She's Father's aunt. She lives in Charlottetown, and she's awfully old. I knew she was coming to visit for a month, but she never tells us exactly when she'll arrive. Oh, she will be so furious!"

Miss Josephine Barry did not appear at breakfast the next morning. Mrs. Barry went in to see her. After she came out, she spoke to Diana quietly in the parlor.

When Diana came back into the kitchen, she looked very serious. "Aunt Josephine says I'm the worst-behaved girl she ever saw," she told Anne. "She says she's not going to pay for my music lessons the way she had promised. She says my parents ought to be ashamed of the way they brought me up. She says she won't stay in this house another day. I don't care, but Mother and Father do."

"Didn't you tell them it was my fault?"

"I'm not a tattletale. Anyhow, it was my fault, too."

"I'm going to tell her myself, then," Anne said. Diana stared.

"Anne, don't do it. She'll eat you alive!"

———

Miss Josephine Barry wheeled around in her chair when Anne walked in. Her eyes snapped behind her gold-rimmed glasses.

"Who are you?" she demanded.

"I'm Anne of Green Gables," Anne said timidly. "It was all my fault about jumping on you last night. It was my idea. Diana would never have thought of such a thing."

"Oh, really? As I remember it, Diana did her share of the jumping."

"But we were only having fun," Anne said. "I think you ought to forgive us, now that we've apologized. Or at least forgive Diana and let her have her music lessons. If you have to be cross with anyone, be cross with me. I'm used to people being angry with me. I can stand it much better than Diana can."

"Do you know what it is like to be awakened out of a sound sleep, after a long journey, by two big girls leaping on you?" Miss Barry said sternly.

"I don't know, but I can *imagine,*" said Anne seriously. "It must have been very disturbing. But imagine how *we* must have felt. We didn't know there was anybody in the bed. You scared us to death. And then we couldn't sleep in the guest room after being promised. You are probably used to sleeping in guest rooms. But imagine how you would feel if you were a poor orphan girl who had never had such an honor."

Miss Barry laughed.

"I guess my imagination *is* a little rusty," she said. "Now, sit down and tell me about yourself."

"I'm sorry I can't," Anne said firmly. "I would like to, because you seem like an interesting person. But I promised Marilla Cuthbert that I would go home first thing. Miss Cuthbert has taken me in. She is trying to raise me properly, but it is very discouraging work. Just please tell me that you will forgive Diana and not go back to Charlottetown."

"Perhaps I will stay, if you promise to come over and talk to me once in a while," said Miss Barry. "You amuse me, Anne-girl, and at my time of life an amusing person is a very rare thing indeed."

Chapter 11

The Daring Game

Soon spring came to Green Gables. Anne and Diana made wreaths of mayflowers and put them on their hats. They walked to school through a vale of violets. The frogs sang in the marshes along the Lake of Shining Waters, and the air was filled with the scent of clover and firs.

Then it was June. Anne had been at Green Gables for one year. She was a star pupil at school, although it was hard work trying to stay ahead of Gilbert Blythe. At home, under Marilla's strict teaching, she was becoming a help and a comfort, especially when Marilla had one of her painful headaches. Anne was even learning to cook.

Anne still made her share of mistakes, of course. Once she emptied a pan of milk into a basket of yarn instead of a bucket. Another time she was daydreaming and walked right over the edge of the log bridge into the brook.

"I know I make a lot of mistakes," she said to Marilla. "But just think of all the mistakes I don't make."

June passed. Mr. Phillips left the school. Anne cried during his farewell speech, even though he had spelled her name without an *e*. But Anne couldn't wait to meet the new teacher in the fall. Her name was Miss Stacy. She would be the first woman teacher Avonlea had ever had.

Anne had a wonderful summer. She worked on her garden and decorated her room with flowers. She went for walks by the sea. She and Diana made up names for all the delightful new spots they discovered. And they scared themselves silly imagining that a ghost haunted the woods behind the house.

Two weeks before school was to begin, Diana gave a party for the girls in their class.

After tea they found themselves in the garden. They were tired of their usual games, so they decided to play "daring."

First Diana dared Ruby Gillis to climb the old willow tree. Ruby did this, even though the tree was covered with fat green caterpillars.

Then Josie Pye dared Jane Andrews to hop around the garden on her left foot. Jane fell down at the third corner, and Josie laughed loudly. So Anne dared Josie to walk along the top of the board fence that surrounded the garden. Josie had no problem with this. When she jumped off the end of the fence, she stuck out her tongue at Anne.

Anne tossed her red braids.

"I don't think it's so wonderful to walk a little, low fence," she said. "I knew a girl once who could walk along the top of a roof."

"I don't believe it," Josie said. "Nobody could do that. You couldn't, anyhow."

"Oh, couldn't I?" cried Anne.

"Then I dare you to do it," Josie said. "I dare you to climb up there and walk along the top of the kitchen roof."

Anne turned pale, but there was only one thing to do. She walked over to the ladder that was leaning against the house. The other girls gasped.

"Don't do it, Anne," said Diana. "You'll fall off and be killed. Never mind Josie. It's not fair to dare someone to do something so dangerous."

"I must do it," said Anne. "I shall walk along that

roof or die trying. If I am killed, you can have my pearl bead ring, Diana.''

Anne climbed the ladder. The girls gathered round and held their breath.

Anne balanced herself on the top of the roof and started to walk along it. She was very high up. She managed to take several steps. Then she swayed and lost her balance. She stumbled and slid down the roof, crashing into the bushes.

All the girls screamed. They ran to Anne, who was lying on the ground, white and limp.

''Oh, Anne, are you killed?'' shrieked Diana.

To the great relief of all the girls, especially Josie Pye, Anne sat up dizzily.

''No, Diana, I am not killed. But I think I am unconscious.''

Anne tried to scramble to her feet, but she sank back again with a sharp cry of pain.

''My ankle,'' she gasped.

<hr>

Marilla was in the orchard when she saw Mr. Barry coming over the hill. He was carrying Anne in his arms. Her head lay limply against his shoulder.

Marilla felt a stab of fear pierce her heart. She hurried down the slope.

"What happened to her?"

Anne lifted her head. "Don't be frightened, Marilla. I was walking along the top of Diana's roof and I fell off. I have probably broken my ankle. But look on the bright side. I could have broken my neck."

Anne's ankle was indeed broken. That night, after the doctor had left, Marilla took a tray upstairs.

"Don't you feel sorry for me, Marilla?" Anne asked sadly.

"It was your own fault," said Marilla as she lit the lamp.

"But that's why you should feel sorry for me. If it were someone else's fault I would feel so much better. Besides, what would you do if someone dared you to walk along the top of a roof?"

"I would stay on the ground and let them dare away," said Marilla.

Anne sighed.

"You have such strength of mind. I haven't. I just couldn't let Josie Pye get the best of me. Now I won't be able to start school with the others. The new teacher won't be new anymore by the time I go. And

Gil—everybody will get ahead of me in class. Just think. If I had been killed, Josie Pye would be known all her life as the girl who caused Anne Shirley's early and tragic death, and—"

"Well, one thing's certain, Anne," said Marilla. "Your fall off that roof hasn't injured your tongue at all."

Chapter 12

$\mathcal{A}$nne Gets Puffed Sleeves

It was October before Anne was able to go back to school.

The new teacher, Miss Stacy, was not like any teacher Avonlea had ever seen. She took her students for nature walks through the fields. She led exercise classes every day. She let them choose their own subjects for their compositions.

When Miss Stacy said her name, Anne just knew that she was spelling it with an *e*.

In November Miss Stacy suggested that the school hold a concert in the town hall on Christmas night. Preparations for a program began at once. No one was more excited than Anne.

Marilla did not approve of concerts.

''It just fills your heads up with nonsense

and takes time away from your lessons," she grumbled.

—

On Christmas morning Anne woke up and looked out her bedroom window. The trees were covered in snow, and the air was nice and crisp.

She ran downstairs.

"Merry Christmas, Marilla! Merry Christmas, Matthew! I'm so glad we have a white Christmas. Green Christmases are never green. They're just nasty faded browns and grays."

Anne suddenly stopped talking. Matthew was unfolding a glossy heap of soft brown material. He held it out to Anne.

Anne could not believe what she saw. "Is that for me?" she asked. "Oh, Matthew!"

It was a dress. The skirt had dainty frills and tucks. There was a little ruffle of lace around the neck.

But the sleeves were the crowning glory. They had long elbow cuffs. Above them were two beautiful puffs decorated with silk ribbons.

"It's a Christmas present for you, Anne," said Matthew shyly.

Anne's eyes suddenly filled with tears.

"Don't you like it?" Matthew asked.

"Like it? Oh, Matthew, it's perfectly beautiful. I can never thank you enough. Look at those sleeves!"

"So this is what Matthew has been grinning about for two weeks, is it?" Marilla said. "I knew he was up to something foolish. There's enough material in those sleeves to make a whole dress. Well, I hope you're satisfied at last. I know how long you've been wanting those silly sleeves. The puffs have been getting more ridiculous every year. They're as big as balloons now. You'll have to walk through the door sideways."

The concert that night was a complete success. The crowded little hall was decorated with evergreen branches and pink tissue-paper roses. Diana sang a solo, and Anne recited two poems. All the performers did well, but Anne was the star of the occasion. Matthew and Marilla were very proud.

"You were awfully mean to Gilbert Blythe," Diana said as the girls walked home. "When you ran off the platform after your poem, one of your roses fell out of your hair. Gilbert picked it up and put it in his pocket. Isn't that romantic?"

"I don't care what that person does," said Anne. "I simply never waste a thought on him."

Chapter 13

Chapter 13

A Perfect Scarecrow

After the Christmas concert, everyday life seemed flat and stale. Anne spent many nights lying awake and imagining the concert over and over. But eventually things returned to normal, and the weeks slipped by. Anne and Diana turned thirteen.

"I cannot believe that I'm in my teens," Anne said. "We know so much more than we did when we were only twelve. In two more years we'll be really grown up. It must be lovely to be grown up, when just being treated as if you were is so nice. When I'm an adult, I'll always talk to little girls as if they were, too, and I'll never laugh when they use big words."

That spring Anne, Diana, Ruby Gillis, and Jane Andrews decided to form a story club. This would help them improve their imaginations and write better compositions. No boys were allowed, although Ruby thought boys would make the club more exciting. Each person had to write one story a week. The girls would read their stories out loud. Then they would talk them over.

Anne told Marilla all about the club. Ruby was very fond of love stories. Diana put too many murders in hers. She never knew what to do with the characters, so she just killed them off to get rid of them.

"I think this story-writing business is the most foolish yet," Marilla said. "You're wasting time that should be spent on your lessons."

Marilla was still very strict with Anne. But in her heart she wondered how she had ever lived before Anne came to Green Gables. As she walked home late one April evening, she looked at the white house happily. She had told Anne to make a fire in the woodstove and set the table. She was looking forward to a warm, cozy kitchen and a well-prepared meal. Anne was finally becoming a good cook.

But when Marilla walked into the kitchen, the stove was cold. The table was bare. There was no sign of Anne anywhere.

Marilla lit the fire and prepared the meal herself. She was very annoyed.

"She's off somewhere with Diana," she muttered. "Writing stories instead of thinking about the time or her chores. She'll have some explaining to do when she gets home."

Suppertime came and went. There was still no sign of Anne. Marilla washed the dishes and put them away. Then she went upstairs to fetch a candle from Anne's room.

She lit it and turned around to see Anne herself lying on the bed. Her head was buried in the pillows.

"Goodness me," said Marilla anxiously. "Have you been asleep, Anne? Are you sick?"

"No. But please go away. I'm in the depths of despair. I don't care whether Gil—I don't care who gets ahead of me in class or writes the best composition anymore. Things like that are not important now because I'll never be able to go anywhere again. Please don't look at me."

"Anne Shirley, what is the matter with you? Get up this minute and tell me. What have you done?"

Anne slid to the floor in tears.

"Look at my hair," she whispered.

Marilla lifted the candle. Anne's hair certainly looked very strange.

"Why, it's *green*!" Marilla exclaimed.

"Yes," moaned Anne. "I thought nothing could be as bad as red hair. But now I know it's ten times worse to have green hair. You have no idea how miserable I am."

"I was expecting something bad to happen. You haven't been in any trouble in over two months. Now then, what did you do to your hair?"

"I dyed it. I knew it was a terrible thing to do. But I thought it would be worth it to get rid of red hair. Besides, I meant to be extra good in other ways to make up for doing something so bad."

"Well," said Marilla. "If I decided to dye my hair, I'd have dyed it a decent color at least. I wouldn't have dyed it green."

"But I didn't mean to dye it green," Anne sobbed. "A peddler came by the house this afternoon. He said he was working hard to make enough money to bring his wife and children from Germany. I wanted to buy something to help him. Then I saw the bottle of hair dye. The peddler said it would dye any hair a beautiful raven black. So I bought it. Now I will never live this down. People have pretty well forgotten my other mistakes—getting Diana drunk and flying into a temper with Mrs. Lynde. But they'll never forget this. Oh, how Josie Pye will laugh. I cannot face her."

"This is what comes of worrying so much about your looks. Well, let's see if a good washing will do any good."

Anne scrubbed and scrubbed her hair. But the dye would not come out.

"It's no use, Anne. We must cut it off. There is no other way."

⎯

The next day Anne's short hair caused a sensation at school. To her relief, nobody guessed the real reason for it. But Josie Pye still had the last word.

"You look like a perfect scarecrow," she told Anne.

Chapter 14

◆

The Unlucky Maiden

The four members of the story club were standing beside the Lake of Shining Waters. They were spending much of the summer there, fishing for trout and rowing around in Mr. Barry's boat.

But today the girls were acting out a poem they had read in school. It was about a beautiful maiden named Elaine, who died of love for a brave knight.

"You must be Elaine, Anne," Diana said. "I could never lie in a boat and pretend I was dead."

"I'd be popping up every minute or so to see where I was," said Jane.

"Well, I'll do it, but it is perfectly ridiculous. Elaine had long flowing hair." Anne's hair was still short, but it looked very pretty. Her head was covered with silky curls held in place by a black ribbon.

Anne climbed into the boat and lay down on one of Mrs. Barry's old shawls. She closed her eyes and folded her hands over her chest.

"She really does look dead," whispered Ruby.

The other girls laid a yellow scarf over Anne. They tucked a flower gently into her hands. Then they pushed the boat away from the dock.

Diana, Jane, and Ruby ran through the woods, across the road, and down the bank. Anne drifted slowly toward the other end of the pond. She was enjoying herself tremendously. It was all so sad and romantic.

Then something happened that was not at all romantic. The rowboat began to leak. In fact, water was pouring through a crack in the bottom.

Anne screamed, but nobody heard her. There were no oars in the boat, and the water was rising quickly.

Just as the boat was about to sink, it floated close to a pile of old tree trunks that held up the bridge. Anne grabbed the scarf and shawl and scrambled out onto the slippery wood. Then she held on tight.

Meanwhile, the boat drifted under the bridge and sank. Ruby, Jane, and Diana, waiting downstream, saw it disappear before their very eyes. They were sure that Anne had gone down with it.

For a moment they stood still, white as sheets. Then, screaming at the tops of their voices, they ran through the woods to Diana's house.

Anne held on and waited. Suppose no one came to help her? Suppose she grew so tired and cramped that she had to let go? She looked down into the deep green water and shivered.

Then, just when she thought she could not hang on another moment, Gilbert Blythe came rowing under the bridge.

"Anne Shirley! How on earth did you get there?" he exclaimed.

He pulled his boat close to the pile and held out his hand. Anne had no choice but to grab it and scramble in. There she sat, wet and furious, with her arms full of dripping shawl. It was very difficult to be dignified.

"We were acting out a poem," Anne said coldly. She did not look at Gilbert. "Would you please row me to the landing?"

When they got to shore Anne sprang out of the boat.

"Thank you very much," she said, turning away. But Gilbert held her arm.

"Anne," he said. "I'm sorry I made fun of your hair that time. I didn't mean to hurt your feelings. Besides, it happened so long ago. Can't we be friends?"

Anne hesitated. Her heart gave a strange little beat. But the scene from two years before flashed into her mind. Gilbert had called her *Carrots.* He had disgraced her in front of the whole school.

She hated Gilbert Blythe, and she would never forgive him.

"No," she said coldly. "I will never be friends with you."

"Fine!" Gilbert jumped back into his boat. "I'll never ask you to be friends again. And I don't care, either!"

He rowed away angrily. Anne headed up the hill. She held her head high, but she couldn't help feeling a little sorry. She almost wished she had answered Gilbert differently.

Halfway up she met the other girls. They hadn't been able to find help, and they were completely hysterical.

"We thought you were drowned," Diana gasped. "We felt like murderers because we made you be Elaine. How on earth did you escape?"

"I climbed up on one of the bridge piles," Anne said. "And Gilbert Blythe came along in a rowboat and brought me to shore."

"That's so romantic," said Jane. "Of course you'll be friends with him after this."

"No, I will not," said Anne firmly. "And I never want to hear the word *romantic* again!"

Chapter 15

—

City Life

"Guess what?" Diana said to Anne. It was a beautiful evening in September, and Diana had just raced over from Orchard Slope.

"Aunt Josephine has invited you and me to town next week. She's going to take us to the Exhibition!"

"Do you think Marilla will let me go?" Anne asked. "She'll say I should be at home studying instead."

"Let's get my mother to ask her. That way she'll be more likely to say yes. We'll have the time of our lives, Anne. We've never been to the Exhibition before."

"Well, I'm not going to get my hopes up," Anne said.

But Marilla did agree to let Anne go to town. The day of the trip the girls got up before sunrise. It was a half day's drive to Charlottetown, but Anne enjoyed every minute of it. The air was fresh and crisp as they rode through the misty valleys in the early red sunlight.

It was almost noon when they reached Miss Josephine Barry's mansion. The big house was set back from the street. It was surrounded by trees. Aunt Josephine met them at the door.

"So, you've come to see me at last, Anne-girl," she said. "And you're so much better-looking than you used to be, too."

"I'm so glad you think so. I know I'm not as freckled as I used to be, but I didn't dare hope that there was any other improvement."

Aunt Josephine's house was like a palace, filled with velvet carpets and silk curtains. But Anne didn't feel very comfortable in such a grand house. It was full of too many things, and all the things were so splendid.

"There is no room for the imagination here," she told Diana. "That is one good thing about being poor. There are so many more things you can imagine about."

They spent all the next day at the Exhibition. Anne

had never seen so many people. She loved the horses and flowers. She was even happy when Josie Pye won first prize for her knitted lace.

The girls went up to the grandstand and watched the horse races. They saw a man go up in a hot-air balloon and had their fortunes told for ten cents each. Anne's fortune said she would marry a dark-haired, rich man and go across water to live. After that she looked carefully at all the dark-haired men she saw, but she didn't care for any of them.

Then the girls slept in Aunt Josephine's guest room. It was an elegant room, but somehow it wasn't as exciting as Anne had thought it would be. That was the worst thing about growing up. The things you had wanted so much when you were little didn't seem half so wonderful when you finally got them.

On Thursday the girls had a drive in the park, and in the evening Aunt Josephine took them to hear an opera singer. Anne had never heard such heavenly singing. It made her feel the way she felt when she looked up at the stars on a clear night.

After the concert they all went to a restaurant for a late-night ice cream.

The girls enjoyed every minute of their trip to

town. Diana felt she was born for city life. But in the end Anne decided that as a regular thing she would rather be at home, asleep in her own room. Even in her sleep she would know that the stars were shining outside and that the wind was blowing in the firs across the brook.

Chapter 16

The Queen's Class Is Organized

Just before Christmas Miss Stacy organized a special class for her advanced students. Every day this group stayed after school to study for the entrance examinations into Queen's, the teachers' college in Charlottetown. Anne was thrilled to join the class.

Marilla and Matthew wanted Anne to have the best education they could afford to give her. Marilla firmly believed that a girl should be able to earn her own living. Unfortunately, Mr. and Mrs. Barry did not, and would not give Diana permission to join the class.

On the first afternoon the Queen's class remained in school for extra lessons, Diana walked home alone. Anne watched her best friend disappear down the path, and a lump came into her throat. She quickly buried her head in her text-

book. She didn't want Gilbert Blythe or Josie Pye to
see the tears in her eyes.

The students threw themselves into their studies. It
gave them a purpose in life, although everybody's
plans were different.

"Ruby Gillis only wants to teach for a few years
until she gets married," Anne told Marilla. "But Jane
Andrews says she's going to be a teacher forever and
never marry. She says you get paid for teaching, but a
husband doesn't pay you anything."

Anne didn't know what Gilbert Blythe's plans
were. Ever since she had refused to make friends with
him by the pond, Gilbert had completely ignored her.
He talked and joked with the other girls. He exchanged books and walked home with them. But he
simply ignored Anne.

Anne told herself that she didn't care, but she did.
In her heart she knew that she was no longer angry
with Gilbert, but it was too late. Instead they were
fierce rivals in class, both determined to be in first
place.

The winter days slipped by like golden beads on the
necklace of the year. There were lessons to learn,
books to read, pieces to practice for choir. Then,

almost before Anne realized it, spring and summer came again to Green Gables. Another school year was over.

Anne and Diana were fourteen years old now. In some ways this was their last summer of childhood. They walked, rowed on the pond, picked berries, and dreamed to their hearts' content. Mr. Barry even took them to the White Sands Hotel for dinner one evening. The dining room was elegant, with fresh flowers and real electric lights.

When September came, Anne was eager to study again. But as the examinations drew closer, her heart sank into her shoes. Suppose she did not pass? In her dreams she could see the list of examination results. She imagined finding Gilbert Blythe's name at the very top, and not finding her name on the list at all.

In the meantime, there were sleigh rides, concerts, and skating parties. Anne grew several inches, until she was even taller than Marilla. She turned fifteen.

And then the time for the entrance exams arrived. Students from all over Prince Edward Island went to Charlottetown. They wrote six examinations in three days. Then there was nothing left to do but wait for the results.

One evening, the news came. Anne was sitting by the open window of her room, admiring the beautiful summer evening.

She saw Diana come flying down through the woods, over the log bridge, and up the hill. Diana held a fluttering newspaper in her hand.

Anne sprang to her feet. Her head was spinning and her heart was beating faster than it ever had. An hour seemed to pass.

Finally Diana burst into the room.

"Anne, you've passed," she cried. "You and Gilbert are tied for first!"

Anne used up half a dozen matches before her shaking hands managed to light the lamp. Then she snatched up the paper.

There was her name at the very top of a list of two hundred. That moment was worth living for.

Anne and Diana hurried down to the field where Matthew was bringing in hay. Mrs. Lynde and Marilla were talking by the lane fence.

"I always knew you could beat them," Matthew said happily.

"You've done pretty well, I must say, Anne," said

Marilla. She was trying very hard not to show how proud she was.

"I guess she has done well, and I'm not afraid to say it," said Mrs. Lynde heartily. "You're a credit to us all, Anne, and we're all proud of you."

Chapter 17

The Hotel Concert

"Wear your white dress," Diana said firmly.

Anne and Diana were in Anne's room. It was no longer the bare, lonely room that Anne had slept in that first night at Green Gables. Pale green curtains fluttered in the window. The walls were covered with dainty apple-blossom wallpaper. Anne had hung a photograph of Miss Stacy on the wall. Below it she kept a little vase of fresh flowers. There were a white bookcase filled with books, a wicker rocking chair with a cushion, and a dressing table with a white frilly skirt.

Anne and Diana were busy getting ready for a concert at the White Sands Hotel. The most talented people in the area were going to perform, and Anne had been asked to represent Avonlea. It was a very great honor.

"The blue one is too stiff and dressy." Diana had excellent taste in clothing, and tonight she was devoting herself to making Anne look wonderful. She tied Anne's sash, put up her hair, and tucked a small white rose behind her ear. Finally Anne put on the pearl necklace Matthew had bought her.

"There," Diana announced. "All ready."

Anne looked very different from the frightened little girl Matthew had met at Bright River. She was tall and slim. Her freckles had disappeared, and her hair had indeed turned an attractive reddish brown, just as Mrs. Lynde had predicted.

The road to White Sands was full of buggies. Laughter and voices echoed everywhere. The hotel was a blaze of light from top to bottom.

As she looked at the other performers, Anne suddenly felt shy and frightened. Her dress seemed too simple. Her pearl beads and single rose seemed plain next to the diamonds of the other ladies.

Anne stood in a corner and wished she were back at Green Gables.

Things were even worse on the platform of the hotel concert hall. The electric lights were dazzling. Anne was seated between a fat lady in pink silk and a tall, snobby-looking girl in white lace.

"What fun it will be to hear all these country bumpkins display their talents tonight," the girl said to the person sitting on her other side. Anne believed she would hate that white-lace girl forever.

Then Anne's name was called. She got to her feet and moved dizzily to the front of the platform. She was so pale that in the audience, Diana and Jane clutched each other's hands nervously.

Anne could not move. Everything was so strange— the rows of ladies in evening dresses, the fancy audience. She felt miserable. Her knees trembled and she began to feel faint.

Then, just as she was about to run off the stage, she saw Gilbert Blythe, sitting beside Josie Pye.

Anne drew a long breath and flung her head up proudly. She would not fail before Gilbert Blythe. Her fear vanished, and she began to recite the poem she had prepared. In a steady, clear voice, she spoke as she never had before.

When she had finished, there was a burst of applause. Then there were cries of "Encore, encore," until she stood up and recited another short piece.

It was a wonderful evening. Anne was introduced to everybody. They all had an elegant supper in the big dining room.

At the end of the evening, as the buggy rumbled along the shore road back to Avonlea, Anne breathed in the pure night air and listened to the murmur of the sea. She knew then that she would never trade places with any of those rich ladies with all their diamonds. She was quite happy to be Anne of Green Gables, with her simple string of pearls.

Chapter 18

A Year at Queen's

The day finally came for Anne to go away to teachers' college. Diana cried when she said goodbye. Marilla did not, but late that night she wept, too. Her Anne had grown up. She would never be a little girl again.

At the teachers' college in Charlottetown, Anne's days were busy. But at night she returned to a narrow little room in a lonely boarding-house, and she was very homesick. The paved street and the telephone wires outside her window were so far away from the great outdoors of Green Gables.

But Anne didn't have time to stay homesick for long. She was trying to get her first-class teacher's certificate in one year instead of two. And she dreamed of winning one of the school's major prizes, the gold medal or the Avery scholarship, which would pay for four years at the university.

Anne worked hard. Her rivalry with Gilbert Blythe was as strong as ever. She made new friends, although no one took Diana's place. She ate Sunday dinner at Aunt Josephine's. And when she could, she went home to Green Gables on the weekends and holidays.

Then, almost before anybody realized it, spring had come and it was examination time. On the morning the final results were posted, Anne was pale and quiet as she walked to school.

When she went up the steps, she found the hall full of boys. They were carrying Gilbert Blythe on their shoulders. "Hurrah for Gilbert Blythe, Gold Medalist!" they yelled.

For a moment Anne felt sick with disappointment. And then somebody called out, "Three cheers for Miss Shirley, winner of the Avery!"

⟶

Anne returned to Green Gables a few days later. Diana was there to meet her. They sat in Anne's room, where Marilla had set a flowering rose on the windowsill. Anne drew a long breath of happiness.

"I have three months of vacation before I go to the university," she told Diana. "By then I'll have a brand-new set of ambitions to aim for. That's the best thing about ambitions. As soon as you achieve one, you see another one glittering higher up. It does make life seem so interesting."

"Miss Stacy has left the Avonlea school. So Gilbert Blythe is going to teach here next year. His father can't afford to send him to the university, so he'll have to earn his own way through."

Anne hadn't known this. She felt a little disappointed. She had thought Gilbert would be going to the university, too.

What would she do without her friend the enemy?

Chapter 19

$\sim$

A Bend in the Road

Anne came through the hall with her arms full of flowers. She was going to put them in water. Then she would get to work making dinner. Marilla was looking tired, and her headaches were getting worse. Anne had decided to spend the summer doing the housework so that Marilla could rest.

She stopped suddenly when she saw Matthew standing by the porch door. He had a newspaper in his hand, and his face was gray. Anne dropped her flowers. She and Marilla ran to him at the same moment. Before they could reach him he had fallen to the floor.

Anne sent for the doctor, but Mrs. Lynde arrived first. She pushed Anne and Marilla gently aside and laid her ear over Matthew's heart.

Tears came into her eyes, and she shook her head.

"I don't think we can do anything for him," she said softly. "Look at his face. When you've seen that look as often as I have, you know what it means."

When the doctor came he said that death had been quick and painless. It had probably been caused by a sudden shock. The shock was in the paper Matthew had been reading. It told of the failure of the Abbey Bank—the bank that held all of Matthew and Marilla's savings.

All day friends and neighbors came and went. But when the calm night came, the old house was quiet and still. Anne fell asleep, worn out by the day's pain and activity. In the middle of the night she awakened. The darkness closed in around her. Then the tears came, and Anne wept her heart out.

Marilla heard her. She came in, and she and Anne held each other.

"What will we do without him?" Anne sobbed.

"We've got each other, Anne. I don't know what I'd do if you weren't here. I know I've been strict with you, but don't think I didn't love you as much as Matthew did. It's never been easy for me to say things out of my heart. But I love you as if you were my own flesh and blood, and you've been my joy and comfort ever since you came to Green Gables.''

➤

Several days after Matthew was buried, Anne came home from visiting Diana. Marilla was sitting at the kitchen table with her head in her hands.

''What's wrong, Marilla? What's happened?''

''I went to see the eye doctor today. He says if I don't give up all work that might strain my eyes, I'll be blind in six months. I can't run this place like that, even with hired help. I am going to have to sell Green Gables.''

''Sell Green Gables?'' Anne wondered if she had heard right.

''If I don't sell, the farm will get so run down that no one will want to buy it. Every cent of our savings was in the Abbey Bank. Mrs. Lynde has offered to let me live with her. At least you have your scholarship, Anne. I'm sorry you won't have a home to come to on your vacations, but—''

''You won't have to sell Green Gables. I'm not going to the university.''

''Not going to the university?'' Marilla looked at Anne in astonishment. ''What do you mean?''

"I'm not going to take the scholarship. I couldn't leave you alone in your trouble after all you've done for me. I'm going to teach. I know Gilbert Blythe has been given the school here, but I can have the Carmody school. I can live here and drive over and back in warm weather. In winters I'll stay there during the week and come home on weekends. I'll read to you and do all the sewing and anything else you can't manage. We'll be cozy and happy here together."

"I can't let you give up the scholarship," Marilla said.

"You can't stop me. I'm sixteen years old and stubborn as a mule, as Mrs. Lynde once said."

It was Mrs. Lynde herself who brought Anne the most surprising news of all a few days later.

"You've been hired to teach at the Avonlea school, Anne," she said.

Anne sprang to her feet. "But I thought they had promised it to Gilbert Blythe!"

"They did. But as soon as Gilbert heard about your plans, he withdrew his application and suggested they hire you. He knows how much you want to stay with Marilla. He is going to teach at the White Sands school. It's very kind of him because he'll have to pay for his room and meals in White Sands. That will make it much harder for him to save up money for the university.''

—

That night Anne went to the little Avonlea graveyard to put fresh flowers on Matthew's grave. Then she walked down the long hill that sloped to the Lake of Shining Waters. Beyond the fields lay the sea, misty and purple.

Halfway down the hill a tall young man came out of the gate of the Blythe house. It was Gilbert. He lifted his cap politely and began to pass. But Anne stopped him and held out her hand.

''Gilbert,'' she said, ''I want to thank you for giving up the school for me. It's very good of you.''

Gilbert took her hand eagerly.

''I'm happy to do it, Anne. Are we going to be friends after this? Have you really forgiven me?''

Anne laughed. She tried unsuccessfully to withdraw her hand.

''I forgave you that day by the pond, although I didn't know it. I've been sorry ever since.''

"We are going to be the best of friends," said Gilbert. "We were born to be good friends."

Marilla looked up curiously when Anne walked into the kitchen some time later.

"Who was that who came up the lane with you?"

"Gilbert Blythe," Anne answered. She was annoyed to find herself blushing.

"I didn't think you and Gilbert were such good friends that you'd spend half an hour talking to him at the gate," Marilla said with a dry smile.

"We haven't been. We've been good enemies. But we have decided it would be much more sensible to be good friends. Were we really there for half an hour? It seemed like just a few minutes. But then, we have five years of conversation to catch up on."

That night Anne sat by her window for a long time. The wind purred softly in the cherry boughs. The stars twinkled over the pointed firs. Diana's light gleamed through the gap in the trees.

Anne sighed contentedly. She still had dreams and ambitions, but she had changed them for the time being. When she had left teachers' college, her future had seemed to stretch out before her like a straight road. Now there was a bend in it.

Anne didn't know what lay around that bend, but

she knew that flowers of quiet happiness would bloom along it.

She would be a good teacher and help Marilla. She would give life her best, and it would give her its best in return.

About the Authors

Lucy Maud Montgomery was born on November 30, 1874, on Prince Edward Island, Canada. Her childhood on the island later inspired her most popular and beloved novel, *Anne of Green Gables,* which was published in 1908. In 1911 she married Reverend Ewan MacDonald; they settled in Toronto and had two sons. Before her death in 1942, L. M. Montgomery had written more than twenty books, including seven more books about Anne, and the Emily of New Moon trilogy.

Shelley Tanaka has written and edited a number of works about L. M. Montgomery and the Anne books, including *The Anne of Green Gables Diary*. She is the author of several books for children and young adults, including *The Illustrated Father Goose, On Board the Titanic,* and *Discovering the Iceman*. She lives near Kingston, Ontario.